P9-DVQ-303

BALLPARK® Mysteries 16

THE COLORADO CURVEBALL

Also by David A. Kelly

BALLPARK MYSTERIES®

#1 *The Fenway Foul-Up*

#2 *The Pinstripe Ghost*

#3 *The L.A. Dodger*

#4 *The Astro Outlaw*

#5 *The All-Star Joker*

#6 *The Wrigley Riddle*

#7 *The San Francisco Splash*

#8 *The Missing Marlin*

#9 *The Philly Fake*

#10 *The Rookie Blue Jay*

#11 *The Tiger Troubles*

#12 *The Rangers Rustlers*

#13 *The Capital Catch*

#14 *The Cardinals Caper*

#15 *The Baltimore Bandit*

#16 *The Colorado Curveball*

SUPER SPECIAL #1 *The World Series Curse*

SUPER SPECIAL #2 *Christmas in Cooperstown*

SUPER SPECIAL #3 *Subway Series Surprise*

SUPER SPECIAL #4 *The World Series Kids*

THE MVP SERIES

#1 *The Gold Medal Mess*

#2 *The Soccer Surprise*

#3 *The Football Fumble*

#4 *The Basketball Blowout*

Babe Ruth and the Baseball Curse

BALLPARK® Mysteries 16

THE COLORADO CURVEBALL

by David A. Kelly

illustrated by Mark Meyers

A STEPPING STONE BOOK™
Random House New York

This book is dedicated to Mrs. Barbara Werner, one of my biggest superfans and supporters. I may not hit it out of the park every time I get up to bat, but it's wonderful to have a fan like Mrs. Werner cheering me on from the sidelines!
—D.A.K.

"I want people to expect more from me because I expect more. If you don't set goals high, you're not trying."
—Todd Helton, Colorado Rockies first baseman, 1997–2013, five-time All-Star, four-time Silver Slugger, and three-time Gold Glove winner

Visit us on the Web!
rhcbooks.com

Educators and librarians, for a variety of teaching tools, visit us at
RHTeachersLibrarians.com

Library of Congress Cataloging-in-Publication Data
Names: Kelly, David A., author. | Meyers, Mark, illustrator.
Title: The Colorado curveball / by David A. Kelly; illustrated by Mark Meyers.
Description: New York: Random House, [2020] | Series: Ballpark mysteries; 16 | "A Stepping stone book." | Summary: Cousins Mike and Kate investigate after someone threatens to tamper with the scoreboard right before the Colorado Rockies' season opener.
Identifiers: LCCN 2019005046 (print) | LCCN 2019007803 (ebook) |
ISBN 978-0-525-57898-7 (trade) | ISBN 978-0-525-57899-4 (lib. bdg.) |
ISBN 978-0-525-57900-7 (ebook)
Subjects: | CYAC: Baseball—Fiction. | Colorado Rockies (Baseball team)—Fiction. | Cousins—Fiction. | Colorado—Fiction. | Mystery and detective stories.
Classification: LCC PZ7.K2936 (ebook) | LCC PZ7.K2936 Fr 2020 (print) |
DDC [Fic]—dc23

Printed in the United States of America
10 9 8 7 6 5 4 3 2 1

This book has been officially leveled by using the F&P Text Level Gradient™ Leveling System.

Random House Children's Books supports the First Amendment and celebrates the right to read.

Contents

A Surprise on the Elevator

Kate Hopkins stuck out her tongue. Soft white flakes drifted into her mouth and instantly disappeared.

"Snow?" she asked. "On the opening day of baseball season?"

"Don't worry," her cousin Mike Walsh replied. "Big Bill, the Rockies pitcher, can definitely bring the heat!"

"He'll need a flamethrower for this field," Kate said. "You can't even see the grass or baselines!"

Kate was right. The Colorado Rockies' field was white with snow. It looked like the middle of winter, but it was early April. Mike and Kate were in Denver with Kate's father for the opening-day game against the Los Angeles Dodgers.

"Maybe we can solve the mystery of the missing field!" Mike said.

Kate shook her head. "We're pretty good detectives," she said. "But I don't think the Rockies will need us to find the field. All they have to do is turn on the heater."

Mike glanced at the thousands of empty, snow-covered seats. He looked past the mountain-shaped scoreboard to the Rocky Mountains off in the distance. "This place is huge," he said. "There's no way they can heat it up fast enough."

Kate smiled. "I'm not talking about heaters

for the stadium," she said. "I'm talking about heaters under the field! The Rockies installed over forty-five miles of heating wires to keep the grass warm enough to grow, since it gets so cold up here in the mountains."

Fans wearing winter coats and hats had started to file into the stadium for the game. Down on the field, the grounds crew ran out to the infield with shovels. They started pushing piles of snow to the sides. Underneath, a big tarp covered the infield grass.

Kate's dad, Mr. Hopkins, laughed quietly. "Well, I guess I've seen it all now," he said. Mr. Hopkins was a scout for the Los Angeles Dodgers. He and Kate's mother were divorced, but he often invited Mike and Kate to meet him on his baseball trips. They had flown in from Cooperstown, New York, while he had traveled from his home in Los Angeles.

Moments later, the sun peeked through the clouds. It lit up the snow and instantly made things feel warmer. The fluffy flakes at their feet started to melt.

Mike used his sneaker to push some snow into a small pile. "Aw . . . why does it have to melt?" he asked. "If we had just a bit more, we could have gone snowboarding and skiing right here!" He jumped into his snowboard stance and held his arms out like he was cruising down a mountain. He bent back and forth as he pretended to carve through the snow. "That would have been real double play—baseball and snowboarding!"

"Didn't you get in enough snowboarding yesterday?" Kate asked. The three of them had spent the day skiing and snowboarding west of Denver. "You're the one who wanted to stop early in the afternoon."

"I didn't want to stop," Mike said. "I just wanted to get hot chocolate and rest."

Mr. Hopkins nodded. "The altitude around here tires you out more quickly unless you're used to it," he said. "That reminds me. Look at that!"

He pointed to the row of purple seats that went all around the stadium, up near the top.

"The purple seats!" Kate said. "That row is exactly one mile above sea level!"

Mike stood up from his snowboard crouch. "I can't wait to try sitting there," he said. "From one mile up, I should be able to see everything in the world!"

Mr. Hopkins laughed. "It's one mile above sea level, Mike," he said. "Not one mile above everything else around here!"

A buzz came from Mr. Hopkins's pocket. He reached in and pulled out his phone. "It's a message from the Rockies," he said. "The game's been delayed by one hour because of the snow. I guess we should look around for some hot chocolate while we wait."

"With marshmallows!" Kate said.

They ran up the stairs to the main walkway and headed for the nearest food stand. Mr. Hopkins followed. Mike and Kate ordered hot chocolate while Mr. Hopkins bought a coffee.

To keep warm, they walked around the stadium with their drinks.

Mike slurped up all his marshmallows first, while Kate stirred hers into the cocoa. "I knew I should have asked for extra marshmallows," Mike said.

Kate laughed. "*Extra* should be your middle name," she said. "Or maybe *More*!"

Mike scowled. "Or maybe *Super Nice*," he said.

Mr. Hopkins's phone rang. "Excuse me, it's George," he said. George was Mr. Hopkins's friend and the engineering manager for the Rockies. He had agreed to meet Mike and Kate before the game. Mr. Hopkins walked closer to the field and answered the phone. Mike and Kate continued sipping their drinks.

"Mmm, this is good," Kate said. She tilted the cup and finished her hot chocolate.

Mike slurped up the last of his. He dropped the empty cup in a trash can and wiped some chocolate from the corner of his mouth. "Now what?" he asked.

Kate's dad was still on the phone.

"How about a quick race now that we're fueled up?" Kate asked. She pointed to the elevator at the far side of the entrance hallway. "First one to push the button wins!"

"Okay, go!" Mike said. He took off running.

Kate dashed after Mike and soon passed him.

They ran neck and neck until they were just a few steps away from the elevator. Then Mike leapt forward and pushed the button. It lit up.

"I won!" he panted.

Kate stopped and nodded. “Yup,” she said softly.

They were just about to turn and head back when the button flicked off.

DING!

The elevator doors whooshed open. Mike and Kate stepped back.

ROARRRRRRRR!

A deafening growl filled the area.

Before Mike and Kate could move, a giant dinosaur came out of the elevator and headed straight for them!

A Troublemaker for the Rockies

Mike and Kate jumped back.

The dinosaur charged forward.

ROAR!

Kate grabbed Mike's arm. "Hang on," she said. "That's not a real dinosaur. It's Dinger!"

Dinger the dinosaur stopped in his tracks. His big head swiveled from Mike to Kate.

ROAR!

He let out another loud bellow. But Kate stepped in front of him.

"Roar, yourself!" she said. "We're not afraid! You went extinct over sixty-five million years ago! You're just the mascot for the Rockies."

Dinger stopped charging at Mike and Kate. His head dropped. He leaned back and held out his hands. His arms were short, and he had one small horn on his nose and two horns poking up from the top of his head. He was purple from head to toe.

"Look at that!" Mike said. "A purple *Triceratops*!" He nudged Kate. "I think he wants to be friends!"

Dinger nodded. He reached out and shook hands with Mike and Kate.

"There are tons of dinosaur bones and fossils in Colorado and some are worth a lot of money, like millions of dollars," Kate said to Mike. "I read about them on the plane ride here. That's one of the reasons they made Dinger the dinosaur their team mascot. But do you know the other reason they did that?"

Mike glanced at Dinger. The dinosaur held up his small hands and shrugged.

"Um, no," Mike said.

"Because they found a *Triceratops* bone when they built the ballpark!" Kate said. "Right under the Rockies' dugout!"

Dinger raised a hand to his mouth as if he was shocked.

Mike smiled and reached out to Dinger for a high five. "I'd say that's pretty cool," he said. "Sounds like good luck to me."

Dinger nodded happily. He gave Mike a high five and danced around a little bit, swinging his tail out behind him and waving his short arms in the air.

A woman next to Dinger motioned to her watch. Dinger bowed to Mike and Kate and waved goodbye as he followed the assistant off down the hall.

"We have to go, too," Kate said. "We're supposed to be meeting George!"

Mike and Kate raced back to her dad, who watched as the workers shoveled the field. The sun shone bright, and the snow on the seats and walkways had turned to puddles.

"There you are!" Mr. Hopkins said. "Just in time. George said he could meet us now. Let's go!"

Mike, Kate, and Mr. Hopkins walked through the stadium to the lower level. Mr. Hopkins showed a security guard his identification. The security guard waved them on.

They walked down a hallway with unpainted gray cinder-block walls. They passed an open door on the left labeled FIELD HEATING SYSTEM. Two men in blue construction suits were inside unpacking some tools.

Mike looked at the unfinished ceiling covered with wires, pipes, and heating ducts above them. Two medium-size TVs on the wall played a pregame baseball show. "Cool! Look at this! We're getting a behind-the-scenes tour of the Rockies' stadium!" he said.

Mr. Hopkins laughed. “We are,” he said.

As they reached the end of the hallway, a stocky man wearing a purple Rockies warm-up jacket appeared.

“George!” Mr. Hopkins said. “Great to see you! This is Mike and Kate. I just told them how you’re in charge of something pretty important here in Denver.”

“That’s right!” George said. He took a ball out of the pocket of his warm-up jacket and tossed it to Mike. “Here’s a gift for you.”

“Baseballs!” Kate said.

Mike turned the ball around in his hand to check it out.

“You won’t *see* anything different about baseballs here, but they are different,” George said. “When we first opened the stadium in 1995, players were hitting too many home runs!”

“So what did you do?” Kate asked.

“The players were hitting more home runs because the ballpark is one mile above sea level and the air is thinner up here. There are fewer molecules of oxygen, which means less air resistance to slow balls down when they’re hit. But more importantly, the mountain air dries out the baseballs, so they’re harder and slicker. That makes it harder for pitchers to grip and throw curveballs and most other pitches. And

drier baseballs also bounce off the bat more than moist ones and travel farther. All that added up to too many home runs!"

"I read about that," Kate said as she pointed to the silver door behind George. "You're the one who found a way to fix it with a humidor!"

George nodded and patted the door. "That's right. I came up with the idea of putting the baseballs in this humidor," he said. "A humidor is kind of like a big refrigerator, but instead of keeping the baseballs cold, it keeps them moist."

Mike tossed the baseball in the air and caught it with his other hand. "So you keep the baseballs in a humidor and add moisture to them," he said. "The moisture makes it easier for the pitchers to grip the balls and put more spin or movement on them. The added moisture also means that the balls bounce off the bat a little less, so they don't go as far."

"Exactly," George said. "Once we started using a humidor, the home run totals for the park dropped to normal levels. Now other teams are starting to use them, but we were the first. Do you want to see inside?"

"Yes!" Kate said. She tugged on Mike's shirt and jumped up and down.

George waved them forward to a large metal door and unlocked it with a key. When he pulled the door open, moist, cool air drifted out.

Mike and Kate stepped into the room-size humidor first. Mr. Hopkins and George filed in behind them. Racks stacked with large flat boxes of baseballs filled the room's shelves. But then Mike spotted something odd in front of them.

"Uh-oh!" Mike said.

"That doesn't look right," Kate said.

George pushed forward to look.

The floor was covered with baseballs!

Several dozen boxes of brand-new baseballs had been knocked from the shelf on the left. The shiny white balls had rolled all over. The empty boxes lay flipped open on the ground.

"That's impossible," he said. "No one's allowed in this room but me. Someone's trying to make trouble for the Rockies!"

A Big Hit

"I *thought* something strange was going on," George said.

He bent down and started putting the baseballs back into the empty boxes. Mike and Kate scrambled to help. Halfway through the cleanup, George stood up and looked at the door latch and lock. "I'd better get this changed in case someone else has a key," he said. "We can't take any chances with the balls. First the note, and now this."

"Um, what note?" Kate asked.

George patted the pockets of his jacket and then reached into his back pants pocket. He pulled out a folded piece of paper and handed it to Kate. She read it out loud to Mike and Mr. Hopkins.

George—

We can't explain now, but we need you to keep an eye on the main scoreboard during the games this week. No one will be hurt, but something is going to happen. You need to be there to see it. We'll explain this fully in a week or two.

Signed, the REAL ROCKIES

Mike let out a low whistle. "Wow," he said. "That doesn't sound good. What are you doing about it?"

George shook his head. “We’ve told the police, and they’re watching the stadium. I’ll be near the scoreboard for all the games this week,” he said. “But now I’m worried about the humidor and the baseballs.” He scratched his head.

Kate nudged Mike. “Maybe we can help,” she said. “We’re good at solving mysteries. You watch the scoreboard, and we can keep an eye on the humidor.”

George glanced at Mr. Hopkins, who nodded. "They are good at mysteries," he said.

George smiled. "Okay," he said. "That'll help me out a lot. I'll let Donna, the guard, know you'll be down to keep an eye on things." He looked at his watch. Then he handed Kate a business card. "I have to go get ready for the game, but here's my phone number. Call me if anything comes up."

"Thanks," Kate said. "We'll check the humidor and hallway every couple of innings once the game starts."

George slipped the last box of balls back onto the shelf and stepped outside. Once everyone left, he locked the door to the humidor.

George led them down the hallway. He waved as he passed the field heating system room that Mike and Kate had spotted earlier.

"Oh, hi, Regina!" he called to one of the construction workers inside.

A curly-haired woman wearing blue coveralls waved back.

"That's the control room for the forty-five miles of heating wire we have under the field," George said to Mike and Kate. "Regina and her team have been here for weeks making sure it's working for opening day."

When they reached the end of the hallway, George spoke to the security guard. Then he turned to Mike and Kate. "Call me if you see anything," he said. "Thanks for the help!" George turned and headed off to check on the scoreboard.

"And I've got a few things I need to do, too," Mr. Hopkins said. "I'll meet up with you after the game."

Kate gave her dad a hug, and he headed off

to do his work. It was getting closer to game time, and Mike and Kate could hear thousands of fans pouring in for opening day. Mike and Kate walked back up to the main walkway. The sun was out. The field was now bright green grass with no hint of snow. Players tossed baseballs to each other, and some ran sprints. Crowds of fans, still in winter jackets, filled the seats.

"Hey, look at that," Mike said. He pointed to small piles of snow that had been pushed into the edge of the warning track next to the field. "This field is perfect for a special play today. Do you know what play I hope we see?"

Kate studied the snow and then shook her head. "Um, no . . . ," she said.

"A snow-cone catch!" Mike said. "That's when the fielder catches the baseball way up near the top of the webbing, and the upper part of it pokes out of the glove like the shaved ice at the top of a snow cone!"

Mike jumped up and pretended to snag a baseball out of thin air. "Got it!" he said. Then he stuck his tongue out and licked an imaginary snow cone. "Mmm, mmm! Cherry!" he said with a smile. He rubbed his belly. "That was good. Let's go find our seats so we can wait for an amazing play!"

Kate and Mike wound through the stadium until they reached their seats behind the Rockies' dugout. The stadium was almost full when the announcer came on the loudspeakers to start the pregame ceremony.

Mike nudged Kate and pointed to the giant scoreboard in center field shaped like a mountain. "What's up with George's note?" he said. "Do you think someone is going to do something to the scoreboard?"

“I don’t know,” Kate said. “What do you think happened with the baseballs?” She took a small tube of lip balm out of her pocket and rubbed it on her lips.

“I don’t know that, either,” Mike said. “If he’s the only one with a key, it didn’t happen from inside the room.”

“Maybe someone stole his key ring and made a copy of the key,” Kate said. She was about to slip the lip balm back into her pocket when she stopped. “And I just thought of a way to test if someone else has a key!”

"How?" Mike asked.

"With this," Kate said. She held the tube of lip balm up in front of Mike. "This is basically wax. All we have to do is put a little of it over the keyhole in the lock on the door. If someone slips a key in, the wax will be pushed into the lock. It won't hurt anything, but we'll be able to tell if someone else uses a key!"

"Great idea!" Mike said.

"We can do it after the first inning," Kate said.

A short time later, the Rockies took the field. Big Bill was pitching for the Rockies. He looked like an old-time train engineer, with a long flowing beard and small dark eyes. The crowd jumped to its feet and roared when Big Bill struck out the first Dodgers player.

But Big Bill got behind in the count on the next batter. With three balls and two strikes, he threw a fastball down the middle. The Dodgers batter swung hard and nailed a long line drive toward the right-field fence. The Rockies outfielder ran as fast as he could for the warning track. The ball sailed over the base path and outfield. The fielder held his glove up high and zoomed to the edge of the outfield. The ball started to drop down just as the Rockies player crossed the warning track.

"Oh no!" Kate said. "He's going too fast! He'd better slow down!"

It was too late!

The Rockies right fielder turned to look for the ball, but he was headed straight for the wall.

BAM!

He smashed into it!

A Secret Behind the Door

The ball dropped behind the outfield wall for a home run!

The wall shook from the force of the right fielder crashing into it.

The player crumpled to the ground.

The runner circled the bases and crossed home plate. Dodgers fans cheered.

"Wow! I hope he's all right!" Mike said. "He hit that *really* hard! Did you see that piece of padding fly off from the back of the wall?"

Kate nodded. She bit her bottom lip and watched as the Rockies center fielder ran over to check on his teammate.

A trainer ran to right field. The crowd grew silent. The trainer leaned down and said something to the player. Then he slipped his hand under the man's back and helped him sit up. The crowd cheered.

A moment later, the man stood. The crowd cheered some more. He waved and walked off the field with the trainer.

Music blared over the loudspeakers. The Rockies players started tossing balls to each other until a replacement outfielder bounded out of the dugout and headed for right field.

The music stopped. Mike watched as Big

Bill stared down the next batter and waited for the catcher's sign.

"I'm glad he's okay," Mike said. "It seemed like he crashed pretty hard."

"Yeah, it *was* pretty hard," Kate said.

"It's like that toy you have," Mike said. "The one with the five steel balls in a line. You lift a ball on one side and let it clack against the ones in the middle. Then the ball on the far side swings up!"

"That's called a Newton's cradle," Kate said. She loved science. "It shows the law of conservation of momentum, or the energy in a moving body. The law says that when two things hit each other, the total momentum before and after the impact is the same."

"Exactly," Mike said. "That's what happened with the runner! When he crashed, his energy got transferred to the wall and knocked

that piece off the back! Boom!" Mike pretended to catch a baseball and knocked his shoulder into Kate's.

"Hey, watch out!" Kate said. She pushed Mike back.

He slumped into his seat. But then he sat up straight. "Maybe that's how the baseballs fell to the ground," he said.

"What do you mean?" Kate asked.

"What if someone wasn't inside the room at

all?" Mike said. "What if the balls fell from the shelf because someone bumped into the wall really hard from the room next door? A really hard bump might have knocked the boxes off the shelves to the floor. Just like your Newton's cradle!"

"Wow, I think you've got something there," Kate said as she stood up. "We saw those construction workers in the room next door. Maybe they bumped into the wall. Let's go check it out."

Kate and Mike ran up the steps to the main walkway and back to the hallway leading to the humidor. When the security guard saw them, she waved them on.

As they ran, their footsteps echoed in the empty hallway. They stopped in front of the door marked FIELD HEATING SYSTEM, which was now closed.

Kate held her finger up to her lips to tell Mike to be quiet. They stood and listened for a minute near the door.

"I can bring another load to the dumpster in half an hour," a man's voice said. "I think we only have two more left."

"Let's knock!" Mike said. He stepped up to the door and knocked. The voices stopped.

Kate and Mike heard some scurrying inside and a sliding noise, like a table being moved.

Kate raised her eyebrows. "Try again," she said.

Mike knocked again, even louder than before. He pulled his hand away and shook it. "Ouch!" he said. "Maybe that was *too* hard!"

The door swung open.

Regina, the construction worker they'd seen earlier, stood in the doorway.

"Hello," she said. "Are you lost?"

"No," Mike said. "George showed us around earlier. We're trying to help him figure something out. I'm Mike, and this is my cousin Kate."

Regina looked from Mike to Kate. "Okay, well, I'm Regina," she said. "How can I help you?"

Kate spoke up. "We wondered if we could see what you were working on," she said. "He said this room is where you control the heaters under the field."

Regina glanced over her shoulder. "Um, sure," she said. "Come on in. But we need to get back to work soon."

Mike and Kate stepped into the room. Construction tools were piled near an empty bookcase on the other side of the room. In the middle of the room sat a pile of something covered in a cloth. Boxes of electrical wires were stacked in the corner. To Mike and Kate's right,

two men in blue coveralls leaned against a closet door.

"That's Parker and Ronan," Regina said. The two men smiled and waved. Parker had curly hair and a Rockies baseball cap. Ronan had straight blond hair and glasses. "We've been doing some repairs on the heating system to make sure it will work correctly."

"So do you have to dig under the field to fix the wires?" Mike asked. "Imagine if you did that and dug a hole for the Dodgers' first baseman to drop into at just the right time! You could win the game by making the other team disappear!"

Regina laughed. "That's a clever idea, but I think it's against the rules," she said. "And no, we're not digging under the field." She pointed to a big box mounted on the left wall. "We've been updating the control box all week."

Kate nodded.

Mike pointed to the far end of the room at the wall that was near the humidor. "Do you mind if I look at the wall down there?"

Regina shrugged. "Oh, sure, no problem," she said.

As Mike walked across the room, he stepped around some shovels and trowels lying on the floor. When he reached the far wall, he scanned it for a moment. He found what he was looking for just to his right, about waist-high.

There was a wide black mark, like something had rubbed against the wall.

Mike pointed to the mark. "Did something hit this recently?" he asked.

Regina stared at Mike for a moment and then glanced at the spot. "Oh, maybe," she said. "We were doing work here yesterday." Regina turned to Parker and Ronan. “Do you remember anything hitting that?”

“Yeah, I think so,” Ronan said. “Yesterday morning we were moving a table and hit that spot pretty hard. But everything seemed okay. Why?”

Kate walked over to look at the mark. “Some of the boxes of baseballs in the humidor were knocked to the floor,” she said. “If something hit here hard, it might have knocked the baseballs off the shelf!”

"That must be it," Regina said.

Mike nodded. "George will be happy to know that no one broke into his humidor!" he said.

"I'm sure he will," Regina said. "But now that you've figured it out, we'd love to get back to work."

"Sure," Kate said. She and Mike headed for the door. They stepped into the hallway, and Regina closed the door behind them.

"We did it!" Mike said. "We solved the mystery of the spilled baseballs!"

Kate glanced over her shoulder at the closed door.

"We might have solved *that* mystery," she whispered to Mike. "But I just discovered *another one*."

"Huh?" Mike asked.

"What are Regina and her workers hiding from us?"

Why Waste a Good Idea?

"What do you mean, hiding from us?" Mike asked.

Kate grabbed his T-shirt and pulled him down the hallway.

When they were far enough away, Kate stopped. "Regina lied to us! She said that they were just working on the control panel and they weren't digging under the field," Kate said. "But there were shovels and trowels on the floor in front of the bookcase! And the sides and back of her coveralls had dirt all over them! That dirt didn't come from the control box!"

"Unless it controls worms!" Mike said with a smile. "But why would she lie to us? She works here. She doesn't need to hide anything."

Kate poked him in the chest with her finger. "Exactly!" she said. "Something is fishy in there."

Mike glanced at the closed door and hallway beyond. "If that's the case, we need to think of a way to get back in there to check things out," he said. The hallway was basically empty. At the far end stood a large trash can. After that, the hallway turned to the right.

"I know how to sneak back in!" Mike said. "I overheard one of Regina's workers saying he had to bring something to the dumpster in half an hour. Follow me!"

Mike led Kate down the hallway, past the humidor door. They stopped in front of the trash can.

"We can spy on them from here!" Mike said. "And sneak back in when he goes to the dumpster!"

"It's not big enough to hide behind," Kate said. "If someone passes by, they'll see us!"

Mike smiled. "We're not spying on them from *behind* the trash can," he said. "We're spying on them from *inside* it!"

Kate leaned over and gave a big sniff. "*Pee-yew!* That stinks! There's garbage in there," she said. "I'm not going to stand in a pile of garbage!"

Mike shook his head. "We don't have to," he said. "Watch!" He took the red plastic top off. A black plastic bag lined the bin. Mike reached in and picked up the bag. He pushed the air out of it and tied it up tightly. Then he dropped it behind the bin.

"All set! No more smell," he said. "Hop in!"

"Okay," she said. "I'd hate to see one of your good ideas go to *waste*!"

"Hey!" Mike said with a smile. "I'm just trying to *clean* this place up!"

Kate climbed into the trash can. Mike grabbed the top and followed her. It was a tight squeeze, but he pulled the top back on. By lifting the flap, Mike and Kate could easily see the door to the field heating system.

"Now we wait!" he said.

Mike and Kate crouched, watching for someone to enter or leave the field heating system room.

"How long?" Kate asked.

Mike let the flap down. It was completely dark inside the trash can. "Let's give it half an hour," he said. "I might need to take a snack break after that."

Kate lifted the flap. The hallway was empty and quiet.

They waited.

Mike fidgeted and kept moving, until Kate pointed out the TV on the wall near the corner of the hallway.

"Cool! At least we can catch the game while we're in here!" Mike whispered. They kept one eye on the TV and one on the door. Big Bill recovered from the home run he gave up and started striking out one batter after another, inning after inning. In the third inning, Josh Devlin from the Rockies swung at the second pitch and hit a home run.

Mike nudged Kate. "He tied the game up!" he said. "Just one more run and the Rockies will be ahead. If Big Bill continues pitching like that, they'll win!"

But even though the Rockies were lighting up the ballpark, there wasn't anything happening down below.

Mike and Kate continued to wait.

And wait.

CLICK!

Mike and Kate held their breath.

The door to the control room opened.

A large moving cart jerked into the hallway. It squeaked as it moved. Parker, Regina's worker with the baseball cap, pushed it.

"Whatever's in there looks heavy," Kate said.

"I know," Mike said.

Squeak!

Parker left the door open and pushed the moving cart down the hall toward the trash can. *Squeak! Squeak! Squeak!* Kate let the flap drop, and she and Mike stayed as still as they could. *Squeak! Squeak!* The cart and Parker passed by them.

The squeaking grew softer.

Mike lifted the flap. Parker had turned the corner and pushed the cart to the end of the hall. They could hear him emptying buckets of something into the dumpster.

"Come on, now's our chance!" Mike said. He quietly but quickly lifted the top off the trash can. Kate climbed out and Mike followed. They ran down the hallway to the open door and stood behind it. Then they peeked into the room.

There was a big pile of dirt on a cloth in the middle of the floor. The empty bookcase had been slid to the right to reveal a large hole in the wall. The hole seemed to lead to a tunnel under the field! They saw no sign of Regina or Ronan.

"He must be throwing away dirt!" Kate whispered. "That looks like the entrance to a mine! I read all about mines in the book about Colorado." Kate liked to study up on places before she went on trips.

"Where's Regina and Ronan?" Mike asked.

"They must be in the tunnel," Kate said.

Squeak! Squeak! Squeak!

Kate nudged Mike. "Parker is coming back!" she said. "We've got to do something before we get caught!" She pointed to a closet opposite the entrance to the tunnel. "Quick, head for the closet!"

Kate and Mike zipped across the room and ducked into their new hiding spot. Luckily, the doors opened *into* the closet. Mike and Kate could stay out of sight behind them, even if one of Regina's workers reached for something inside.

A moment later, Parker and the squeaky cart came into the room. He pushed the cart near the pile of dirt and started filling it up again. When it was full, he wheeled the cart down the hall to the dumpster.

As Parker left, Kate glanced around the edge of the half-open closet door at all the tools near the tunnel opening: a pickax, two shovels, an assortment of chisels, a bunch of brushes with black bristles, a plastic bottle of liquid, a tape measure, and a hammer with a pointed tip. Then she looked at the entrance to the tunnel.

"I think I figured out what they're digging for in there," Kate said.

"What?" Mike asked.

"Gold!"

Locked Up!

"Gold?" Mike asked.

Kate nodded. "Yup, *oro*!" she said. Kate was learning Spanish and liked to practice speaking it. "Gold! Look at all this stuff. Pickaxes, chisels, shovels, and a mining entrance! Colorado is loaded with gold and silver deposits. There are old gold mines all around Denver. They must have discovered gold when they were working on the heating wires!"

"Wow, cool," Mike said. "Maybe we could

find some, too, and get rich. If I had all the money in the world, I could pay someone to do my homework and I could drink PowerPunch all the time! I'd be the king of Cooperstown!"

"I don't know about that," Kate said. "If you had all the money in the world, I think you'd be more like the giant of goofing off! But we're not going to take any of the gold. We need to get out of here to tell security."

"Yes," Mike said. "And then we can solve the second mystery! We need to figure out why someone's threatening to do something to the scoreboard!"

Squeak! Squeak! Squeak!

Mike and Kate hid behind the closet door as Parker and the cart came back into the room. He pulled up the cloth from the floor and put it in the corner. Then he ducked into the tunnel.

Kate tapped her finger on the floor. "I've

been thinking about that," she said, "and I have a theory. What if Regina sent that note?"

"Regina?" Mike asked. "Do you think Regina or her workers are going to do something to the scoreboard, too?"

Kate smiled. "No! That's the whole point!" she said. "Nothing's going to happen to the scoreboard."

"Then why did they send George that note?" Mike asked.

"Because they wanted him far away from all this digging!" Kate said. "If he spent the whole game watching the scoreboard, they could keep digging without anyone figuring out what they were doing! If George had seen them throwing away dirt, he would have been curious."

Mike nodded. "That's a pretty good theory," he said.

"We should tell security," Kate said.

"Let's go," Mike said. "As long as they're still in the tunnel, we can sneak out the way we came in. I'll get to the door first and open it. Make sure to close it really quietly after you go through it."

Kate gave him a thumbs-up.

"It's go time," Mike said. He was just about to sprint for the door when he heard voices from the tunnel.

Kate tugged on his shirt. "It's too late," she said. "They're coming!"

Mike pulled back.

They quickly ducked behind the closet door and watched through the crack near the door's hinges.

The voices grew louder. A moment later, Regina, Parker, and Ronan walked through the tunnel entrance. They carried a large piece of plywood with something on it. They placed it on top of the cart and then stepped back.

"Okay, that's it," Regina said. "Let's cover it."

The two men grabbed a large cloth and put it over the board on the cart.

"Perfect," Regina said. "We're almost there. Let's put these tools away and get rid of the evidence."

Regina, Parker, and Ronan scurried around the room cleaning up. They dumped the tools

into a large canvas bag, swept up the dirt, and pushed the empty bookcase back in front of the tunnel.

"Good job! Now let's get this to the truck and get out of here," Regina said. She headed for the hallway door.

"Okay," Parker said.

They started to head for the door, but then Ronan stopped. He pointed to the closet door. "Hang on," he said. "Let me close that."

Mike and Kate pulled away from the door.

"He's coming!" Kate whispered. "What do we do?"

Mike pushed her flat against the wall of the closet. "Shh!" he whispered. "Don't move!" He also stood flat against the wall and held his breath.

They heard Ronan's footsteps as he approached the door. They even saw the brown leather work boot on his foot as he grabbed the handle of the door and pulled it shut!

Mike and Kate stood against the wall holding their breath in complete darkness.

They could hear the *clump-clump* of the man's boots as he walked away.

Kate exhaled. Mike let out a sigh. "Whew! That was close," he whispered.

"Yes, it was," Kate said.

They heard the door to the hallway open. A moment later, they heard it shut.

"They're getting away with the gold!" Mike said.

Kate grabbed the doorknob and tried turning it.

It wouldn't budge.

"It's stuck!" Kate said.

Mike fumbled for the doorknob in the darkness. He tried to turn it hard to the side. But it wouldn't move.

His hands dropped from the doorknob.

"It's no use," he said. "We're locked in!"

No Bones About It

Kate tried the doorknob again. It wasn't turning at all. The blackness of the closet seemed to be closing in.

"We've got to get out of here!" Kate said. "They're stealing the gold!"

Mike fumbled in his pocket. He pulled out his phone and turned on the flashlight. It lit up the closet. He held it close to the door and looked at the doorknob.

"Hey!" Kate said. "Why don't we call George

and tell him what's going on?"

"Great idea," Mike said. He dialed George's number, but nothing happened. Mike tried again but didn't hear a ringtone. He shook his head. "It's no use. There's no signal. We can't call anyone!"

Kate sighed. "Then we've got to get out of here ourselves," she said.

"What if we break the door down?" Mike asked. "Look around for anything we can use to punch a hole in it. Then maybe we can reach out and turn the knob to open the door."

They scanned the closet area as Mike moved his flashlight over the shelves. They were all empty except for a screwdriver and a carton of napkins.

"Dead end," Kate said. "And that's where we'll be if we don't find a way out. No one even knows to look for us here!"

“There’s always a way out,” Mike said. “We just haven’t found it yet!”

“I know,” Kate said. “It just felt like a good time to be dramatic.”

Kate dropped to the floor and peeked under the door. She could make out the wheels of the moving cart they had seen earlier.

Mike nudged her foot with his sneaker. “Hey,” he said. “I have an idea.”

Kate popped up and moved away from the door.

“I saw my dad do this once when he painted my bedroom door,” Mike said. “Maybe it will work here.”

Mike grabbed the screwdriver from the shelf and put the blade against the top hinge of the door. Then he pushed at the thick metal pin that held the hinge together. It slid up about two inches. Mike reached up, pulled it out, and showed it to Kate. It was about four inches long and looked like a thick nail.

"The pins hold the two hinge plates together," Mike said. "They allow the door to swing open. If we can get the other one out, we can pull the door down!"

Mike went back to work on the bottom hinge. A moment later, he popped the pin out.

"Got it!" he said. He dropped both pins on the floor. "Now give me a hand."

Kate stood near the doorknob so she could lift that side of the door up. Mike stepped over to the hinge side and used the screwdriver to pry the side of the door off the hinges.

The right side of the door dropped slightly, but Mike caught it and pulled backward. Light flooded the closet. Kate grabbed the doorknob. The door came out of the frame.

Mike and Kate lifted the door and set it down against the wall outside the closet.

The doorway was completely open!

They were free!

"Good job!" Kate said.

She gave Mike a high five, and then they stepped into the room. It was empty. The cart

loaded with gold was gone. Regina and her workers were nowhere to be seen.

"We don't have much time," Mike said. "Let's get out of here and warn George."

"No," Kate said. "That would take too long. They'll be gone by the time we talk with George. Our only hope is to stop them in the parking lot! I think there's an exit at the end of the hallway, near the dumpster."

Kate and Mike ran out the door and down the hall. They passed the trash can where they'd hidden earlier and rushed for the door marked EXIT. On the way, they passed rooms marked UMPIRES, MASCOT, and STORAGE.

Kate pushed open the exit door, and they bounded into bright mountain sunshine.

They skidded to a stop and looked around as their eyes adjusted. In front of them was an employee parking area, filled with cars and trucks. There was no sign of Regina or the workers.

"There's the gold!" Mike said. He pointed to a cart with a tarp, standing against the wall to their left. "They must be getting their truck. We still have time!"

"But not a lot," Kate said. "We have to stop them!"

"We will," Mike said. "But let's get a quick look at what they've found. I've never seen a real gold nugget before." He stepped over to the cart and lifted up a corner of the cloth. He held it high, and then started pulling it back.

"Hey!" Mike said. "There's no gold here!"

"That's impossible!" Kate said. "We heard them digging. They had all those excavating tools."

Mike shook his head. "I don't think that's what they were looking for!" he said.

Kate ran over to the cart.

A bunch of white and brown objects lay on the wood. Kate's eyes lit up.

"Hey, they weren't digging for gold," Kate said. "They were digging for dinosaurs!"

Stopped in Their (Fossilized) Tracks

"They're stealing dinosaur bones?" Mike asked.

"Yes, that's it!" Kate said.

Mike leaned over and picked up a large bone. It looked like an arm bone. "But why steal some old bones?" he asked. "Do you think they run a museum?"

"Because they can be worth a lot of money," Kate said. "Sue, the *T. rex* that was discovered in South Dakota, sold for over eight million dollars!"

Mike let out a low whistle. “Wow,” he said. “Maybe I should take one or two of these, then.”

“Not unless you want to get arrested,” Kate said.

Mike put the bone down. “No, I don’t,” he said. “I think I’ll leave them right here!”

“Good idea,” Kate said. She took out her phone and snapped pictures of the dinosaur bones. Then she covered up the bones and pulled Mike over to the door.

"You stay here and watch for them," Kate said. "I'll go get security. If they return, you need to try to stop them somehow!"

Mike flexed his muscles. "I can do that!" he said. He made a show of inhaling deeply through his nose. "All this fresh mountain air gives me superstrength!"

Kate rolled her eyes. "Well, I don't know about that," she said. "But maybe save your strength to keep them from leaving with those bones!"

Kate tugged the door open and disappeared back inside the stadium. Mike tucked his hands into his pants pockets and stepped off to the side so he wouldn't be seen. In the background, he could hear the announcer for the game call out the names of the batters as they stepped up to the plate. A few minutes later, he heard a roar go up from the crowd.

"Another run for the Rockies!" the announcer boomed. "Now they're ahead by three!"

"Woo-hoo!" Mike said softly as he looked around for a TV screen. But instead of finding one, he spotted Regina and her crew driving up for the bones in a pickup truck! He glanced at the door. There was no sign of Kate or security yet.

He stepped behind a pillar. The truck stopped in front of the cart. Parker and Ronan hopped out of the truck and walked around to the back. Parker clicked the tailgate open and lowered it. Regina stepped out and inspected the back of the vehicle.

"We have to be careful loading our cargo in so it doesn't get damaged," she said. She directed the men to spread out a stack of blankets piled in the back. They took their time, carefully covering the bed of the pickup.

Mike glanced at the door again, but with no sign of Kate, he started to sneak over to the pickup truck. "Maybe I can let the air out of their tires while they're loading the truck," he said quietly to himself. Mike headed for the outside front of their truck, where they wouldn't see him. But before he could get there, the door to the stadium exploded open.

ROARRRRRRRR!

A purple dinosaur charged out of the stadium and straight for Regina and the pickup truck! Parker and Ronan jumped back. Regina ducked behind the side of the truck.

The dinosaur spun to its left and made slashing motions with its giant purple hands.

But when Mike looked more closely,

something was strange. The dinosaur didn't seem to have a body! It was all head, hands, and big white feet. It also looked awfully short for a dinosaur.

What's going on? Mike thought.

The dinosaur twirled around and gave Mike a thumbs-up.

It was Kate!

A smile spread across Mike's face. He gave Kate a thumbs-up back and then dropped down near the front tire of the truck and started to let air out.

PFFFFFT!

Mike popped up as air started leaking out.

"You dummies!" Regina yelled to Parker and Ronan. "It's just a kid! Let's get our stuff and get out of here."

As Regina's workers tried to grab the cart and pull, Kate took hold of the other side. But her dinosaur gloves were too slippery, and Parker and Ronan easily tugged the cart away from her.

Kate dropped the gloves, pulled off Dinger's head, and stepped out of the big white dinosaur feet. She ran between the cart and truck and said, "We're not going to let you take things that don't belong to you! You can't just steal a multimillion-dollar dinosaur skeleton!"

"Wrong!" Regina said. "We *are* stealing a multimillion-dollar skeleton, and you're not going to stop us!"

Parker and Ronan simply stepped around Kate to load the skeleton into the back of the pickup truck. Mike jumped in and tried to help Kate, but Parker and Ronan brushed both of them off. When the two workers finished, they covered the bones with a heavy tarp and hopped into the truck.

Mike and Kate tugged at their door, but Parker had locked it.

Regina slammed the driver's-side door shut and revved the engine. As she started to drive forward, the truck pulled sharply to the left because of the tire that Mike had flattened. Regina punched the brakes.

"Got ya!" Mike yelled. He gave Kate a high five. "We stopped them!"

Regina jumped out of the truck and looked at the tire. "What's going on?" she asked.

"We caught you!" Mike called. "I guess we let the air out of your plan!"

Before Regina could respond, the doors to the stadium flew open again.

Three security guards ran into the parking lot and toward the truck.

"Don't move!" the guard in front said. "Nobody steals dinosaurs from the Rockies!"

A Terror-Dactyl

Before Regina, Ronan, and Parker could escape, the security guards rushed over and rounded them up. One security guard stayed behind to guard the dinosaur bones in the truck, while the other two led the three criminals back into the Rockies' stadium.

As the door closed, the security guard nodded to Mike and Kate. "George and the security chief said to tell you to meet them at George's office after the game," she said.

"They want to go over what happened today."

"Sure," Kate said. "No problem!"

The announcer's voice boomed in the background as another player stepped up to bat.

Mike turned to Kate. "If we hurry, we can catch the end of the game," he said. "But what about that?" He pointed to Dinger's head lying on the ground, and the dinosaur hands and feet nearby. "Shouldn't we return it? And where did you get it from, anyway?"

Kate smiled and walked over to the costume. "When I ran into the building, I went to the nearest security phone I could find," she said. "They said they'd send some guards right down. But I was worried that Regina and her crew would get away, so I was trying to think of ways to delay them. When I passed a room labeled MASCOT, it gave me an idea. Luckily it wasn't locked, and there was an extra Dinger costume on the shelf!"

Kate picked up the big feet and hands. Mike picked up Dinger's large purple head. He held it up over his head and let out a roar.

"ROARRRRRR!" he said. "I know that Dinger's a *Triceratops,* but I think you scared Regina and her crew so much, you looked like a *terror-dactyl*!"

Kate laughed. She pulled the stadium door open. "Come on," she said. "We've got to put this away and get back to our seats before the Rockies' game goes extinct!"

A few moments later, Mike and Kate had put Dinger back in the mascot room and made their way to their seats.

The sun shone brightly on the Rockies' stadium. It had warmed up enough that many of the fans had taken off their hats and gloves. Dinger—the real one—danced on top of the dugout roof. The Rockies fans rocked the house because it was the eighth inning and their team was ahead by four runs!

"I'm glad the Rockies are ahead. But what I really want to see is a home run, since it's supposed to be easy to hit one here!" Mike said. "Maybe I could help the Rockies out by going down to the humidor and turning it off. That would make the baseballs drier and lighter. They'd be flying out of this park like popcorn out of a pan!"

"Let's just stay here and watch the rest of

the game," Kate said. "Then we'll meet up with George and my dad at the stadium office."

Mike took a sip of PowerPunch and a bite of his hot dog. They had stopped to fuel up on the way back to their seats. "Okay," he said. "Sounds good to me!"

Marco Jackson from the Rockies stepped up to the plate. The Rockies fans cheered. Mike and Kate clapped along. "Let's go, Rockies!"

Marco swung at the first pitch that crossed the plate.

WHAP!

The ball sailed high into the Rocky Mountain sky. Mike and Kate leapt up from their seats and yelled "Go! Go! Go!" as the ball flew higher. The fielders ran back to the wall as fast as they could.

Marco ran for first. The ball started to drop back down. Marco rounded first and headed for second base as the ball dropped over the wall. The fielders stopped and turned around.

"Home run! Home run!" Mike shouted. "Woo-hoo!" He gave Kate a high five. "That's exactly what I wanted to see. I guess a good hitter can send even a waterlogged ball out of the park."

The fans roared when Marco crossed home plate. The Rockies were now ahead by five.

Mike and Kate dropped back down into their seats. The rest of the game went quickly. The Rockies didn't score any more runs in the eighth. The Dodgers tried to catch up in the ninth inning but only got one runner on base before the Rockies' pitcher struck out three batters in a row.

Game over. The Rockies had won!

Dino-mite!

Mike and Kate cheered with the rest of the fans as the players jogged off the field.

"That was a great end to the game!" Mike said.

"It was, if you're a Rockies fan," Kate said.

"And we're Rockies fans today!" Mike said.

Mike and Kate stood up as the fans around them started to leave. Kate led the way to the stadium office.

They met George in a conference room

with trophies and medals on display. A security guard with a name tag that read PAM sat next to him. Shortly after Mike and Kate walked into the room, Mr. Hopkins arrived.

"What's this I'm hearing about you two and a dinosaur?" he asked.

Kate gave her dad a hug. "Hi, Dad," she said. "We weren't *digging* for trouble today! We just happened to find a multimillion-dollar dinosaur theft in progress!"

George laughed. "I'm not sure if those dinosaur bones will be worth millions of dollars, but they are worth a lot of money," he said. "And Kate's right. She and Mike were the only reason that Regina and her crew didn't escape with expensive bones."

"How did they even know there were dinosaur bones under the field?" Mike asked.

"Well, you've heard the story about how

they found dinosaur bones when they built the stadium, right?" George asked.

Mike, Kate, and Mr. Hopkins nodded.

"Turns out, this is related to that," George said.

"Regina confessed the whole plan," Pam, the security chief, said. "Her father installed the field heating system when the stadium was first built. He's the one who found the original fossil. But what he didn't tell anyone was that he also found a whole dinosaur skeleton."

"He wanted to dig it out himself and get rich by selling it," Pam continued. "Since it was near the field heating system room, he thought he would go back sometime and get it. But he became too sick to work and never made it back. Instead, he left Regina a letter about it when he died and told her how to find it. She waited until the system needed repair and planned on

14

digging it out then. That's what she and her crew have been doing all week. They just didn't think they would be caught by two kids!"

Mike and Kate smiled.

"We were only trying to figure out who spilled the baseballs," Kate said. She nudged Mike with her elbow. "But I guess we *uncovered* a lot more than that!"

"Hey! *I'm* the one who does the puns," Mike said.

"Sorry!" Kate said. "You're not the only one who has a sense of humor. If you're so good, you do one!"

"Okay," Mike said. "I will. What do you call it when a dinosaur has a car accident?"

"I'll bite," Mr. Hopkins said. "I don't know, what?"

"A *Tyrannosaurus wreck*!" Mike said. "Get it? Like a *Tyrannosaurus rex*?"

Mr. Hopkins laughed. “Yes, Mike, I get it,” he said. “And it sounds like Regina and her crew are going to get it, too, for trying to steal the dinosaur. What’s going to happen to it?”

“We’ve already called the museum,” George said. “They were thrilled. They’ll be here tomorrow to help us figure out what to do with it.”

“Great!” Kate said.

“Yes, it is,” George said. “We really appreciate you and Mike helping the Rockies today, so we wanted to give you a token of our thanks.”

Pam stood up and opened the door.

And in walked a dinosaur!

“Dinger!” Mike said.

Dinger came over and gave Mike and Kate fist bumps. He motioned for them to hold out their hands and reached inside a box that Pam held. Then he lifted up a reddish-brown object and dropped it in Kate's hands.

"Is it a dinosaur bone?" Kate said. She held it up and looked at it more closely.

Dinger nodded.

"Cool!" Mike said. "We're rich!"

George laughed. "Not so fast, Mike," he said. "It is a real dinosaur bone from sixty-six million years ago, but it's not going to make you rich.

We found a few bones last year when we did some work on the stadium. The museum didn't want them, so we held on to them. We knew we'd find an important use for them. It's your payment for being such awesome detectives!"

"Thanks!" Kate said. "This is amazing!" She handed the bone to Mike.

Mike took it and held it up in front of him.

"Wow, this is so cool, I *dino* what to say!" Mike said.

George laughed. "We're glad you like it," he said.

"Like it?" Mike asked. "We love it. This gift is *dino*-mite!"

BALLPARK® *Mysteries*

Dugout Notes

☆ Colorado Rockies ☆

Stadium. The Rockies' stadium opened in 1995. It's located in downtown Denver, near a beautiful old train station and lots of restaurants and shops. You can't escape the Rocky Mountains at the Rockies' stadium—they are visible in the distance over the outfield, the scoreboard is shaped like a mountain, and the batter's eye area behind center field is designed like the Rocky

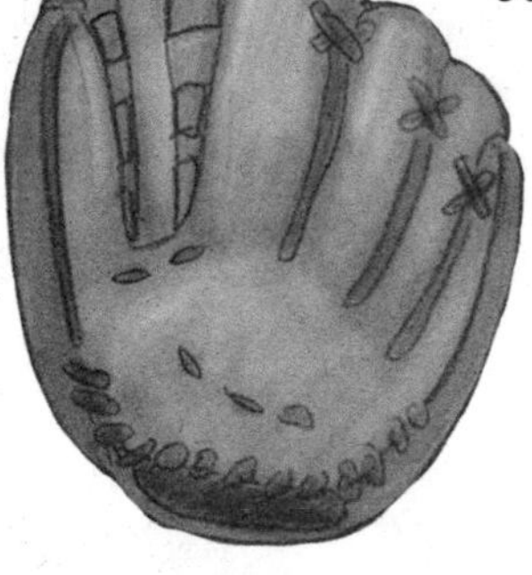

Mountains, with a waterfall, fountains, pine trees, and rocks. The fountains blast water after a Rockies home run!

Dinosaurs. The Colorado Rockies really did find a dinosaur rib bone under their ballpark when it was being built. Millions of years ago, dinosaurs roamed all over Colorado, especially ones like *Stegosaurus, Triceratops,* and some long-necked dinosaurs. Today, there are lots of places visitors can experience dinosaurs in Colorado. Dinosaur National Monument has trails and fossils. Dinosaur Ridge, west of Denver, has self-guided tours of exposed dinosaur fossils (like dino footprints!).

Mining. Colorado was built in large part by people coming to mine its land for valuable minerals and rocks. Gold and silver were found in large quantities in the mid-1800s. In addition, over the years, people have also mined for copper, uranium, iron, and coal. Visitors to the Denver area can tour real gold and silver mines, climb through long dark tunnels, and even dig for gold in some locations!

Trains. Trains are an important part of Colorado history. There are train tracks just outside the Rockies' stadium. Fans sitting near the top can watch (and hear) trains as they go by the ballpark. Railroads are important for moving people and goods, but they also served the mining industry. About an hour west of Denver, visitors can ride trains that snake through the Rocky Mountains and over tall, thin bridges.

One Mile High. Denver is known as the "Mile High City" since it is approximately one mile (5,280 feet) above sea level. As a result, the Rockies' ballpark has the highest elevation in Major-League Baseball. The stadium even has a special row of seats that's exactly one mile above sea level! Almost all other major-league ballparks are fewer than a thousand feet above sea level. Baseballs hit at the Rockies' stadium travel farther than at other stadiums because the air one mile up has less resistance. According to MLB, a baseball can travel 9 percent farther at one mile up than at sea level. A ball hit 400 feet at Yankee Stadium (close to sea level) might travel 440 feet in Denver! The thinner air also means that it's harder for pitchers to control the ball. For example, curveballs will curve less at the Rockies' stadium because there's less air resistance.

Heated field. The Rockies' field was the first major-league field to have a heating system installed under the grass. Sometimes spring comes late to the Rocky Mountains, and the team needed a way to let the grass grow long enough for opening day. They installed a heating system with wires that can heat the soil, so the grass warms up and starts to grow earlier than it otherwise would. It can also help melt the late-spring snowfalls.

Humidor. The humidor at the Rockies ballpark stores baseballs at 70 degrees Fahrenheit and 50 percent relative humidity, similar to the factory environment.

For a long time, the Rockies were the only team that kept its baseballs in a humidor. But now the Arizona Diamondbacks do, and other teams might also. Regular baseballs in drier climates like Colorado and Arizona can be too slick from lack of moisture. Putting the balls in the humidor and adding moisture gives the pitchers more control over them.

Cheap seats. In Denver you can still go to the baseball game for a dollar! Fans under twelve or over fifty-five can buy a ticket for a buck! The seats are in a special section called the Rockpile, behind center field. Everyone else can sit there for $4.

Sherlock Holmes. Part of the idea for this Mike and Kate mystery came from a Sherlock Holmes story called "The Red-Headed League," by Sir Arthur Conan Doyle. In that story, a man is hired to do a pointless job (copying an encyclopedia) because robbers want him out of his shop during the day so he won't hear them digging a tunnel to the bank next door. I used that concept to help shape what Regina does to George in this story with the note about the scoreboard.

Catch the next baseball mystery in

BALLPARK® Mysteries 17

THE TRIPLE-PLAY TWINS

Mike and Kate are in Minnesota for a big Twins game. They're especially excited to see the Torres twins (Marco and Pedro) play! But when Marco starts acting strange and takes off before the first inning, Mike and Kate get ready to investigate. Can the super sleuths reunite Marco and Pedro before it's time to play?

Coming in 2021!

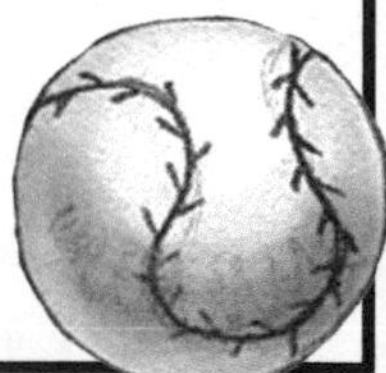

New friends. New adventures.
Find a new series . . . just for you!

RHCB RHCBooks.com

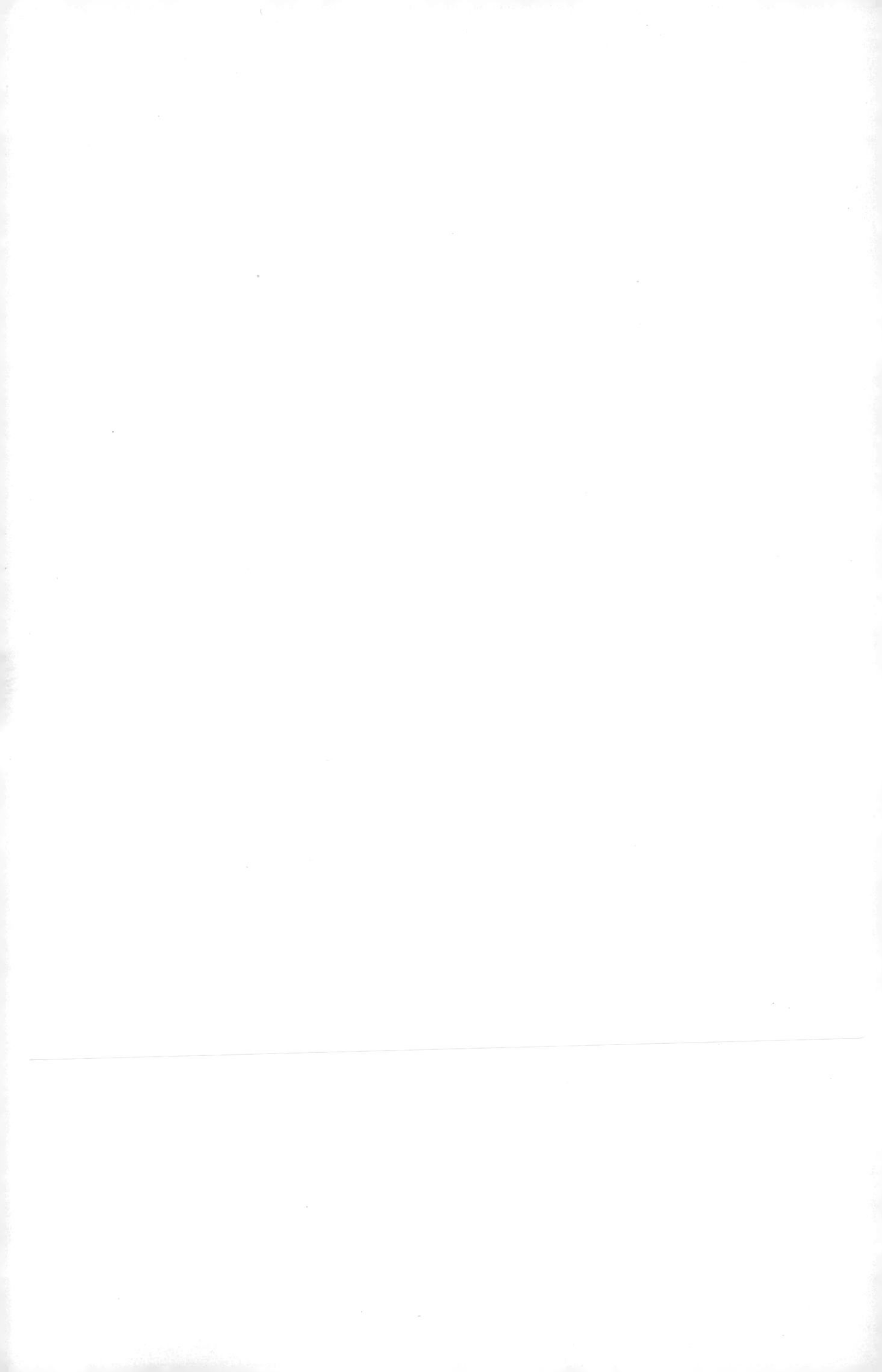